Total

# SO LONG AND THANKS FOR ALL THE BACON...

*"This is the best book I've ever read.*
*It's also the only book I've ever read."*
~ Dottie Lowenstein

*"If bacon is my spirit animal, then*
*Fred Rewey is a grapefruit fork."*
~ Jim Callahan

*"This book was on the other side of the room... I can walk again!"*
~ Julie Swatch

*"Someone left this in the break room,*
*and I couldn't find anything else to read."*
~ Karen Milson

*"Could have used a bit more flair."*
~ Stan

*"I am pretty sure this just came free with my Kindle."*
~ Larry Ellison

*"I like bacon as much as the next gal, but damn!"*
~ Christy Keller

*"I was interested in reading this, but then someone took my copy*
*I left in the break room. I will burn this place down."*
~ Milton

*"Krueger's elegy for innocence is a deeply memorable tale."*
~ Washington Post accidentally misplaced quote for
William Kent Krueger's *Ordinary Grace*

*"This book is wicked awesome. Er-ruh"*
~ Guy trying and failing to nail a fake Boston accent

*"This book was* ███████ *and* ████████████. *It is our*
*recommendation that the reader* ██████, ██████,
*and* ██████████."
~ U.S. Government

*"So Long and Thanks for All the Bacon was a really*
*good book with lots of interesting themes and characters.*
*Anyone who likes books will also like this one"*
~ High School kid who skimmed the cover and needed to
submit an overdue book report

*"Fred will never amount to anything in this world.*
*He is not a team player"*
~ Fred's fourth grade teacher

*"I found this book at a garage sale. Was a waste of a day but,*
*at least I scored a good lava lamp with it."*
~ Bill Wilson

*"This ASTOUNDING new book will*
*TANTALIZE your SENSES, EDUCATE you*
*about BACON and ENTHRALL you with*
*Fred Rewey's SENSE OF HUMOR!"*
~ AutoFakeQuoteGenerator.com

*"With great power comes great responsibility."*
~ Uncle Ben, every single G**D*** time

*"You'll be hearing from my lawyers."*
~ the late Douglas Adams, author of
*The Hitchhikers Guide to the Galaxy*

# So Long And Thanks For All The Bacon...

By Fred Rewey

First Printing, 2019

ISBN-13: 9781701780064


Exposure One
13900 County Road 455
Clermont, FL 34711

Ordering Information:
Quantity sales. Special discounts are available on quantity
purchases by corporations, associations, and others. For details,
contact the publisher at the address above.
Orders by U.S. trade bookstores and wholesalers

www.FredRewey.com


Printed in the United States of America

# This Book is Dedicated To Tracy and Mikayla.

Not only are these the two most important women in my life, but they also have to deal with me in real life – and with all the material that didn't make the book.

# With Special Thanks To...

All my cigar-smoking friends. A unique group of ruffians* that come together and solve the world's problems, go home, only to come back the next day to find it is all screwed up again. It is tough out there. We do our best, after all, it's 'Not all cotton candy and kitten whiskers.'

*I just really wanted to work in the word 'ruffians.'

# ABOUT THE AUTHOR

About once in every decade, a book comes along that changes not only the way you think but also your future take on mankind and its path.

Can you recall a transformative book that made you question the entire meaning of life and rocked you to the core?

**THIS IS NOT THAT BOOK!**

Photo: Thor Nielsen, Cigar Press Magazine

This is a book that some dude, ok me, just felt like it needed to be written. I probably just did it for my inner child who's still wondering why, as an adult, I don't eat ice cream *every* morning for breakfast?

I'm unsure there's anything I can write in the 'About the Author' page that you won't figure out by reading the book.

It's a compilation of thoughts and observations usually running through my head as someone talks to me at a cigar bar, in line at a grocery store, or while pumping gas.

If the randomness of my brain distracts readers in the process…that's probably not surprising. If not, well, at least

I've cranked out another book to support a loose table leg or something when I am old.
I really think many of us just take life too seriously at this point.

If we can't sit around and have fun with each other in a respectful way, then I think humanity is heading down a road that leads to total anarchy...or at least Candy Corn being used as a pizza topping.

Before you get to make fun of someone else, you have to be willing to laugh at yourself...and sadly, many people can't.

The fact of the matter is that in today's day and age, many people focus on the few ways we're different instead of the majority of ways we're all the same.

We all want the same things: a roof over our heads, food on the table, safety, and opportunity for your kids. Anything else is just noise.

I hope you enjoy the book. If so, feel free to shoot me an email, leave a review, follow me on Facebook/Twitter, or buy me a cigar when you see me. Ok, that last part was worth a shot.

All the best,

Fred "@Godfadr" Rewey
Facebook / Twitter / Instagram: @Godfadr

# TABLE OF CONTENTS

# IKEA Meatballs

There are a few stores in the world that I'll avoid at all costs:

**Any store that smells like soap.**

**Any store that has an unusually high number of mannequins!**

**Any IKEA stores.**

For starters, there's no other store that's designed to trap you on the floor for hours more than IKEA.

Not because there's cool shit to see…oh no…because you cannot find your freakin way out!

You know those rooms where people pay to get locked in, figure out puzzles and crud for 45 minutes, to then find a key and be let out of the room?

**IKEA is the original Escape Room!**

*Except…*

…you didn't know going into it that you'd be trapped, you probably don't have friends with you, and there certainly is no guarantee that, at the end of 45 minutes, the IKEA gods are going to let you out and brand you a loser AND that a group of 11-year-olds beat your time by half.*

*\*That last part is purely hypothetical.*

Nope. At IKEA you're trapped until you find meatballs. Which, as far as prizes go, are pretty good.

I did an Escape Room in Lake Tahoe once, sadly there were no meatballs at the end.

But, at IKEA, getting to the meatballs at the end is no easy task. You must first go through endless rooms and fake directional signs.

Each 'mock room' is clearly meant to sell stuff to college dorm students or someone who lives in an 11-square-foot apartment.

Don't get me wrong. IKEA is incredibly efficient at designing for small spaces (or prison cells). If I had an 11-square-foot apartment, I'd do all my shopping there.

Throw in a couple alcoves of couples arguing how to put the shit together, and I think you will have a life-like experience on your hands.

But, back to the meatballs.

I was told by someone that the 'quality' of the meatballs isn't very good.

### Seriously?

Complaining about the quality of IKEAs meatballs would be like saying you refuse to drink a strawberry Yoohoo after 3 days in the desert.

IKEA meatballs are the prizes at the end of the maze!

Prize.

Maze.
Rats.

Cheese.

Meatballs.

I really think our consumer experience at IKEA is a reality show on some alien's computer somewhere.

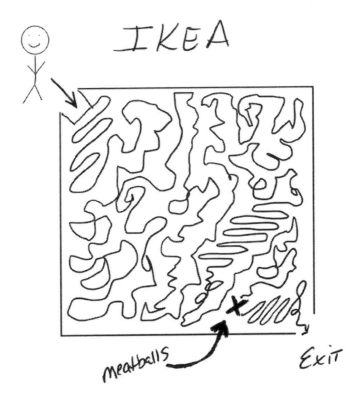

SO LONG AND THANKS FOR ALL THE BACON...

# ALIENS

I don't know who said this, "the fact that Aliens have never contacted us is proof that there is intelligent life out there."

**But I can't argue with it.**

Personally, I think there are aliens out there...somewhere.

For starters, it'd be a really colossal waste of space if there weren't.

I know there are a lot of people who don't believe in aliens, and I'm really unsure why.

I don't know if it comes from vanity that we've got to believe we're the only game in town or something far more deep-seated.*

*Or is it 'deep-seeded' – damn...where is Grammarly when I need her?*

When I brought up the subject to a few of my more religious friends, they were pretty clear that there are no aliens.

Apparently, God spent all week molding us and the planet together, but then He (or She) took Sunday off to watch football and eat French Onion dip.

I'm not exactly sure what he/she did the following Monday...I'm going assume he/she grabbed a pizza and watched *The Bachelorette* or *Dancing With the Stars*.... but religion isn't really clear on how the rest of God's weeks were spent.

**I mean…could God not have built something else?**
Was God really THAT lazy? Just sort of a one-off artist who threw together Earth (with people) and then retired?

It seems like we might've been the first attempt. Or maybe the last? Could go either way.

No reason to deny the fact that there COULD BE life outside our planet.

However, when that fateful day comes, you know, when Aliens come to visit us…

*…shit is going to get real.*

Now, it could go down a couple ways. Here are the 'Fred Rewey Vegas Odds On How We Meet Aliens'

**Respond to Phone Call – Odds 142:1**

We keep sending up satellites, drones, and rockets into space, blasting music or mathematical formulas trying to get someone's attention.

The dreamy-eyed scientists think they'll discover one of these rockets and be eternally grateful that they've found a new Facebook friend.

In reality, we're that loud, obnoxious guy in a Datsun Honeybee who spent four paychecks on a sound system so that everyone driving within 50-yards of him can hear that he likes Chumbawamba[1] at full volume.

In this scenario, aliens contact us with a noise restraining order, also requesting that we stop sending them our naked dick pics.

## Alien Ship Crash Lands On Earth – Odds 4000:1

Odds of this happening again? Crashes are highly unlikely since they no longer allow aliens to text and fly.

## Elon Musk Mishap – Odds 25:1

What most people don't know is that when Elon Musk shot the Tesla into space, there was an alien low-jack feature that offered a $100,000 reward for the safe return of the vehicle.

The wheels will be off, and there'll be illegible graffiti, but a Good Samaritan will return the car back to claim the reward…

…and then destroy the planet.

## They Wait Until We Are Gone – Odds 5:1

Aliens could just sit back and not come down here until we blow ourselves up or overindulge on triple-stuffed Oreos and then swoop down to check out what all the screaming was about.

I suspect the first thing they'll do is tap into the computers and check out everyone's Facebook accounts.

Then, according to everyone's Facebook comments and status updates, the alien race will release how many 'experts' lived on this small blue marble and mourn our extinction.

[1] *Author Note: No disrespect to Chumbawamba…I actually like them.*

So Long And Thanks For All The Bacon...

# BACON

Bacon is awesome. Enough said except…

**Fred Rewey**
@GodFadr

I am worried the FBI is monitoring my bacon consumption.

6:12 AM - 4 Mar 2019

**NSA/CSS**
@NSA

Wrong Department. But don't worry, there is not an "official" bacon watch list. At least as far as you know.

Reply   Retweet   Favorite   More

4:06 AM - 4 Mar 19 · Embed this Tweet

SO LONG AND THANKS FOR ALL THE BACON...

# FLYING CARS AND FLAT EARTHERS

*(Disclaimer: Occasionally, the language in this book may be offensive to some readers. Learning to read is recommended).*

When I was a kid, I was promised flying cars.

**Flying f\*\*\*ing cars!**

As of this writing, I am 52-years-old, and I don't have a flying car.

*\*Full disclosure, this year I turned 53, so this seemed like the best time to write this chapter, while I still have my wits about me. Frankly, this whole aging thing is bullshit. If one more person posts "YOLO" on social media, I'm going snap. YOLO? F\*\*\* you.*

**So, why exactly DON'T we have flying cars, Fred?**

Well, I am glad you f\*\*\*ing asked.

Because Scientists, who I suspect were just about to give us flying cars, have been pulled away to explain to a few dozen people that the Earth is indeed, not flat.

Yes, Virginia, there's a group of people who believe, with all their being, that the Earth isn't round.

*Are these people crazy, Fred?*

Ok, if you really did just ask that...then you just might be part of the problem. OF COURSE, they are f***ing crazy...

...and not a "cool" sort of crazy, like that redhead you dated for 4-days in college. No, we are talking bat shit crazy!

Anyway, here is how it probably all went down in the secret science lair that was...just about...to give us flying cars;

### 9:08 am – Wednesday - Secret Scientist Meeting
### Location: Classified Lair
### Meeting Minutes #45593

**Perkins:** *Fellow scientists, the time has finally come. We are prepared to give the public flying cars.*

**Johnson:** *This is the most remarkable thing we've ever done since our houseboat rave after collecting all that cash from the Nigerian Prince.*

**Perkins:** *Right you are, Johnson. I would also like to take this time to thank Dotty for her contribution to thermal combustion disbursement and also figuring out where to put the Pizza Roll warmer. I only wish we had that figured out before Hal's test drive.*

**Dotty:** *He would've wanted us to move on.*

**Perkins:** *So, without any further delay, let's send this spam email to everyone letting them know...*

**Milton:** *Sir, Wait.... WAIT!*

**Perkins:** *What is it, Milton? It is not Donut Thursday, and we have important work to do.*

**Milton:** *Sir, we have a problem.*

*Perkins: Well, we will just have to deal with it after the flying car launch. Nothing gets in the way of...*

*Milton: Some people think the world is FLAT!*

*Perkins: WTF?*

*Milton: Yes, sir, I checked it out myself. There are posts on Facebook and Twitter. There are numerous blogs about it. There are people who deem the world is flat.*

*\*Dotty Faints\**

*\*Perkins clutches heart\**

*Perkins: Well, f\*\*\*, the flying car is just going to have to wait.*

**And THAT's why I'm pissed at Flat Earthers!**

# THE MCRIB

Few items in the fast-food industry have polarized the American people more than the McDonald's McRib.

**There are only two camps…**

**A: You love it.**

You think it is full of BBQ awesomeness that can only be achieved using some sort of alien technology… or…at the very least, created by Gordon Ramsey during a drunken escapade at Costco.

*Or*

**B: You hate it.**

You think Satan himself put the sandwich on this Earth to see who'd actually eat a sandwich shaped like rib bones in a vile pre-formed manner.

*That's it!*

**There's no middle ground. So, don't even try and find some.**

No one has ever said, "Man, I tried that McRib sandwich yesterday, it was just ok."

Nope. No. One. Ever.

Either you're selling your cousin's kidney for the opening of McRib season or, you're telling your roommate that they are never allowed to leave Yelp reviews online...*for the rest of their lives.*

**So, what got us here? Why do people care so much, either way?**

Well, that's a very tough call.

That's why I've made this handy brief list of "topics" that you might want to run by your family, friends, and significant other, just to see where they stand.

**Think of it as a party game....** *that might end a relationship.*

**McRib** (I'd save this one for after you have warmed up)

**Pizza** (softball, if someone doesn't like pizza then he or she is a sociopath)

**Coke vs. Pepsi** (can't we all just get along?)

**Taco Bell is authentic Mexican food** (the correct answer is 'no')

**Pizza with Pineapple** (this doesn't end well)

**"Sauce" or "Gravy"** (my Italian friends will punch someone over this one)

**Cooking steak above 'medium' temperature** (don't do it)

**Lucky Charms vs. Fruit Loops** (hint: marshmallows always win)

**Cats vs. Dogs** (I included a helpful chapter on this in the book)

**Bacon is Incredible** (this is how you can purge some Facebook friends)

**Best Star Wars Character** (It's a trap!)

I suppose if you can agree on 80% or more, you've found your soul mate!

If you find yourself only agreeing on 20% or less, it's probably time to make some new friends.

← Fred with McRib

← Fred without McRib (and apparently missing a hand)

So Long And Thanks For All The Bacon...

# UBER

This spring I was visiting Las Vegas and took an Uber ride.

It was a routine enough ride. The woman didn't speak much, and I didn't throw up in her car. So, it pretty much adhered to how an Uber ride transaction is supposed to work.

At one point, the driver spoke up and asked me a few questions.

Basically, she overheard my conversation with Tracy regarding nerve endings and Bell's Palsy.

In any case, the Uber driver was fascinated and asked me a bunch of questions. By the end of the ride, she stated, in a bold fashion, that she'd be giving me 5 Stars for my passenger rating.

That prompted me to look up my passenger rating in Uber.

**4.76 Out of 5.0**

Apparently, that's a pretty damn good Uber score, but I can't help but wonder what I did on some Uber rides to not get a 5.0.

Now Uber will tell you, "don't be disappointed if you don't have a perfect score...most people do not."

*Why don't I have a perfect score?*

I decided to turn to the Internet to see what 'bad things' people do to deserve poor ratings. Here are ten in no particular order...

1. Throwing up / Passing out
2. Foul language use
3. Making Uber wait
4. Making drivers go through Taco Bell drive-thru
5. Shooting handgun out of the sunroof
6. Sex with partner
7. Smelling funny / Traveling with offensive food
8. Clipping toenails
9. Changing baby diapers
10. Eating / Drinking

I can safely say that I've never done any of these things.

Although, full disclosure, I should add a couple of these to the Uber bucket list.

I suppose there could be a whole bonus system: like combining #5 and #6, and your next ride is free.

I guess there are some legitimate complaints an Uber driver could have against me.

Then again, I never asked one to take me to IKEA.

# $120 Flip Flops

Yes, I own a pair of $120 flip flops.

Now, before you get all holier than thou on me, let me explain.

**First off, I've got two feet...**

*...and I use them every day.*

I just didn't want you to think I was purchasing something overpriced, and it wasn't going to get used. Like my Mammoth Tusk Cigar Cutter.

I'm pretty partial to my feet...and walking. So, a good pair of shoes always seems like a solid investment.

When I was young, a friend of the family told me you could never spend too much on shoes, belts, ties, or steaks.

In retrospect, he spent most of his life drugged out in Amsterdam...so maybe he wasn't the best role model to bring up here...but anyway...we're already in it so...

If you're into flip flops as long as I've been, then you're always looking for the perfect pair.

OluKai started sometime around 2005 (I think).

They are awesome flip flops, available in full leather, cool stitching, hold up well...blah, blah, blah.

The first time I went to purchase a pair, I found them in a cool little shop.

The pair was bound together by a security cable.

I asked the shoe kid to remove the cable, so I could try them on.

He stared at me blankly like I just asked to lick them.

"You want to try them on?" he asked.

"Yes, $120 for a pair of flip flops you are damn right I am going to try them on." – I said.

He had to get a manager, so I suspect this was either his first week or I wasn't really qualified to be shopping there. It could've gone either way.

**Anyway, I got to try the flip flops on.**

I suspect if walking on fluffy bunnies was something socially acceptable to compare this to...that'd be about right.

They were awesome, so I purchased them.

When I walked out of the store, I realized what I'd done.

Don't get me wrong, I'm not a miser when it comes to my money, but I don't like to waste it either.

The realization that I'd just blown over $100 on a pair of flip flops was starting to sink in. I thought there probably could've been a better use of that money. Tacos. Bacon. Anything.

Who the f*** pays over $100 for a pair of flip flops?

FLIP FLOPS!

But, that kind of thinking passed, and I set off to find a matching belt.

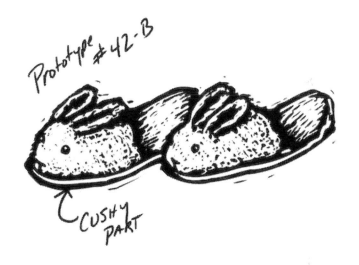

Prototype # 42-B

CUSHY PART

# DEAR WHITE PEOPLE

Dear White People:

I've been stalking you on social media for some time.

For the most part, your posts are amusing and provide us solid distraction from the mundane world of boring status updates.

Your posts on camping, kids, kittens, and back-yard renovations are on point.

However, there are professionals, we call them 'chefs,' that do an outstanding job of creating real works of culinary art.

Not only are these masterpieces amazing to look at *(hint: no filter used in the photo),* but also, they take your taste buds on a journey that cannot be expressed in words.

*Here is the deal…*

Gorden Ramsay, Bobby Flay, Rachael Ray, Alain Ducasse, Alton Brown - they've been trained and schooled for **years**.

They've worked their way up in the ranks after a decade of shitty back-of-the-house jobs prepping shrimp, fish, steaks, or potatoes.

They know food inside and out.

They know the science. They know how to create *and what not to create.*

## YOU ARE NOT ONE OF THESE PEOPLE!

Please, for all that is holy, stop trying.

Your Instagram is filled with things like Tuna and Waffles, Nutella Fish Tacos, Strawberry Couscous, Cheese Stuffed Multigrain Croissants, Jell-O Sticks with Mayonnaise Dip and, let us not forget, Kalemole *(whatever the F\*\*\* that is)*.

*Seriously? What's wrong with you? Stop!*

Why do you feel the need to take a grocery cart full of Wal-Mart frozen foods and attempt to win over Instagram with your cooking skills?

For years now, Pumpkin Spice has been the Fall go-to culinary cop-out.

*Which brings us to an essential public service announcement...*

# WE INTERRUPT THIS BOOK FOR A PUBLIC SERVICE ANNOUNCEMENT

### Save The Pumpkins!

*What if I told you that you'll be key?*

*What if I told you that you can make a big difference?*

*What if I told you that you're all that stands between the thin line of sane and insane?*

**This is a pumpkin field...**

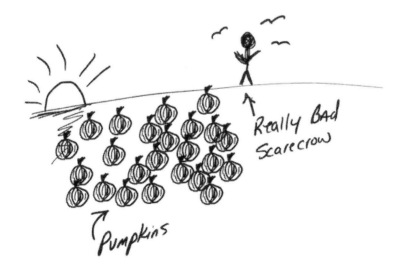

It's one of several around the world with diminishing numbers.

**These are the lucky ones.**

The few that'll never be subject to becoming Hipster drinks, foods, and accessories.

Because these pumpkins are destined for pumpkin pie.

They're the lucky ones.

Many other pumpkins are not as fortunate. Their destiny has been altered by mankind in a grotesque manner.

Robbed of their true calling, these pumpkins are harvested in small cages to create 'pumpkin spice.'

This pumpkin lifeblood is then used in ice cream, Eggo Waffles, potato chips, candy corn, snack bars, breakfast cereals, breakfast yogurt, gum, pop tarts, pop rocks, dog treats, and vodka.

**The list goes on and on.**

I know these things are hard to think about, but we can change the world together.

For only three cents a day, you can sponsor a pumpkin so that it grows up in a safe environment, not being subjected to these gruesome endings.

For less than the price of a donut each week, you can ensure the safety of a harmless pumpkin and help it reach its ultimate god-intended outcome.

**Your pumpkin will be used in pumpkin pie.**

When you sponsor a pumpkin, you'll receive both a photo and a letter from your pumpkin right until the very end.

**Won't you find it in your heart to donate?**

**PeopleForPumpkinPie.com**

So Long And Thanks For All The Bacon...

# Garanimals

Somewhere around 1972, someone invented something that truly benefited mankind.

*No, not the digital camera.*

*No, not the Sony Walkman.*

*No, not the Atari 2600.*

**I'm talking about Garanimals!**

If you're unfamiliar with Garanimals, they were every kid and parent's dream.

They delivered a matchmaking system of style that ensured you never left the house without your clothes coordinating in a pure (and matching) runway-ready style.

The execution was nothing short of simplistic beauty.

You simply matched the 'Garanimals' on the tag from the pants with the 'Garanimals' on the tag from the top.

Tiger pants matched any Tiger shirt.

Any Elephant shirt would flawlessly merge with any Elephant pants.

Just match the Garanimal to Garanimal.

Sure, I suspect there was some trouble making freaks that paired a Monkey with a Panda, or god forbid, a Koala. But those people were rare and probably hung out behind the mall dumpsters.

**There's only one thing that stopped this from being one of the greatest inventions ever...**

Unlike Underoos, there was no reason for adults to outgrow Garanimals.

You only need to ask my wife to understand my lack of style when it comes to picking out clothes.

This extends *beyond* picking out stuff for myself.

My wife will often ask me, "Which one of these outfits should I wear tonight?"

Rest assured, there's about a 93.5% chance whichever one I pick...she ends up wearing the other.

I know, I know, when you see me in person, I look like the guy who has it all together. Style, looks, full head of hair.

What you don't see is an entourage of people behind me keeping me in check.

When I was single, I use to purchase the entire outfits off mannequins.

I assumed, and probably correctly, that someone was paid big bucks to know what to pair together. If it was good enough for the mannequin, it was good enough for me.

My wardrobe is relatively basic.

When I find something I like, I purchase multiples.

I love Cariloha shirts (Gray or Blue)

I like Prana jeans.

I like Olukai flip flops.

My drawers and closet are filled with these items.

Garanimals for adults would've changed all that.

I could've been that well-dressed dude* who picked out his own clothes!

*I say "dude" because let's be honest with ourselves men…we're not very good at fashion. I mean ask us to build a bonfire out of Popsicle sticks and a failed grade-school volcano; we're your guy. Instruct us to not leave the house with a striped shirt, checkered pants, and six-year-old-comfortable-high-tops — not so much.

Maybe you even upgrade the adult line beyond animals?

Maybe you have the **Adult Garanimals: Mid Life Crisis Edition?***

*I highly suspect that edition would be made of boats, cars, tacky tattoos, and some sort of trendy alcohols.

Nope.

We missed out.

Adult Garanimals should've happened.

Till then, when you spot a naked mannequin in the store…it was probably me…but not for creepy reasons.

# TIME TRAVEL

There have been numerous movies and books that involve time travel…

*Time After Time, Groundhog Day, Back to the Future, The Butterfly Effect, Looper, and of course, The Terminator.*

Actors carelessly go forward and backward in time…typically making a mockery of our past trends.*

*\*In all fairness, I really thought the Flock of Seagulls hairstyle would last.*

**But let's focus on the positive.**

When posed with the question of what you'd do if you went back in time, many people respond with obvious answers first…

…invest in Apple

…stop Hitler

…save some of our childhood toys

…take better care of our health

The fact that my future self has never traveled back in time to talk to me proves I'm on the right track - or *that there's no time travel.*

The purpose of this chapter is to simply see if time travel is even possible.

You might go back in time and see if you can still get a refund on this book *(Spoiler Alert: You can't)*.

You might go back in time and purchase MORE copies of this book to give to your friends and family (hint: there is still time).

If you could go back in time, what would you tell your younger self? Other than what we've covered above?

**For me? I'd probably go back in time and tell myself to leave this chapter out of the book.**

# INVENTIONS

I really want to invent something.

I want to be the guest on Shark Tank that has an idea so good Mark Cuban has Kevin O'Leary in a headlock while Lori Greiner drops a studio light on both of them.

I suppose most people want to invent something that's meaningful. Something that helps others.

You know, like cure baldness, stop ingrown toenails, unclog drains, or remove seeds from a watermelon.

I'm just not that ambitious.

I mean, it doesn't have to be something that has mainstream appeal, it just needs to be something where I can say, "I invented that."

I might've missed the boat on these really cool inventions.

**Powdered Milk.**

Some dude was actually sitting around thinking, "damn, you know…milk is really wet. I bet some people want all the benefit of milk, without all that pesky moisture."

*That would've been a good one to invent.*

Did you know there's a **banana slicer**?

Did you know someone invented **Diet Water**?

Did you know that someone actually created a **gas-powered flashlight?**

Yep, those are all pretty useless, but someone, somewhere, thought it was a really terrific invention. Matter of fact, they might've sold a couple.

**So, this brings us to the crux of the issue.**

These items were invented because someone had an actual NEED for these things.

Someone was sitting around thinking how hard it was to cut up a banana.

Another dude was thinking what to do with one leftover piece of pizza, so he invented a zip lock baggie that goes around your neck and stores it (really, you can look that one up).

*I mean let's get real for a second...*

*...who the hell has leftover pizza?*

*Monsters. That's who.*

Anyway, if the invention must come from an everyday need, maybe I need to look at my own life to find something I need?

*I could use a Tator Tot warmer for my car.*

*A Pizza Dispenser in my bedroom headboard for when I get hungry at 3:11am.*

*Something that keeps my hair out of my eyes but isn't a barrette or a 70's headband.*

*A Pez dispenser that throws out warm bacon pieces.*

*A Roomba you can use at parties, but instead of cleaning, it throws out Skittles for everyone.*

**Admit it…that last one sounds pretty festive, huh?**

Anyway, you don't need to worry. I'm not going to invent anything too soon.

But I'm going to keep nagging Elon Musk for that Tator Tot warmer. You know…for all mankind.

# Robots and Automatic Faucets

I don't think, as humans, we're nearly concerned enough about the growing popularity of robots in our lives.

For starters, nearly every movie shows robots turning on humans at some point. That's not 'artistic license.' That's something we all believe.

So, you would think with all the warning signs that we would back the f*** off and stop creating robots that can outrun us?

Nope…we just keep building them.

Sometimes I think no one has ever seen the movie *Terminator*…

…or *Blade Runner*

…or *The Matrix*

…or *2001: A Space Odyssey*

…or *Westworld*

That whole 'robots take over the world' thing is real.

**Oh sure, not yet.**

You can sit in the safety of your own home and tell Alexa to play your **High School Days** playlist and think nothing of her taking over your home one day.

But mark my words.

**It. Will. Happen.**

*Why?*

Because we're stupid.

Ok, maybe not stupid, but robots are smarter than us.*

*So are dolphins and a rare breed of cactus, but that's a story for another day.*

It isn't that we won't see this stuff coming. As a matter of fact, robots are already testing our 'human' limitations.

Remember that time you walked right into an 'automatic' door because it didn't open?

Yep, that was a robot.

That 'spinning wheel of death' on your computer that causes you to lose everything you wrote in chapter two?

Yep, another robot.

Of course, the most common and frequent item robots test us on is the automatic faucets at airports and fancy restaurant bathrooms.

You know, the ones that supposedly have a sensor that knows when our hands are in the sink and starts the flow of water?

Nope…not happening.

No water at all.

You can just stand there with that pine-scented soap on your hand while a group of robots hidden behind the mirror laugh at you.

I'm unsure why the 'water test' is the most important one for robots. There's some pivotal point that will decide who wins the world.

Yes, I believe the fate of mankind will be determined by our ability to turn faucets on or off…at least in the beginning.

In the meantime, fellow humans, stay vigilant, work on your Jedi mind control abilities to turn faucets on and off, and for the love of God, watch EVERY YouTube video that shows robots running, jumping, doing backflips, or stacking stuff in a warehouse…

…it encourages the robots, thereby getting them addicted to how many 'likes' and views they get on social media.

The more time they're chasing 'likes,' the less time they'll have to take over the world.

But just in case, anytime I talk to Siri or Alexa, I say 'Please' and 'Thank you.' – When they take over the world, they'll remember my kind manners and, hopefully, spare me.

# Cheesecake Factory

There are very few food items or restaurants that stress me out.

We've already established that I've no problem with bacon, the McDonald's McRib, and Hamburger Helper.

I like Taco Bell, although I'm not under the delusion that it's even remotely close to real Mexican food.

As a general rule, I tend to avoid buffets, but the concept of them continues to intrigue me.

Any dive open at 3:15 am that's one penalty away from the health department closing them down most likely has the best food.

**So, why is it then that the Cheesecake Factory stresses me out?**

Let's start with the part that they create combinations of cheesecake that no man should ever devise, let alone eat.

I'm a traditionalist when it comes to cheesecake. I like New York style cheesecake.

That's it!

Ok, if you want to throw a few raspberries on it to make it look pretty, I won't kick you out of the house, but that's it.

The second you start throwing on some Chia seeds or something, you are out.

I decided to visit my local Cheesecake Factory and do some serious investigative reporting.

Here are some of their flavors I found in the store and online…

**Low Carb Cheesecake** *(Ok, we're just off to a bad start).*

**Low Carb Cheesecake with Strawberries** *(Am I the only one thinking about that whole 'lipstick on a pig' expression?)*

**Caramel Pecan Turtle Cheesecake** *(I, for one, am not for the senseless killing of turtles nor does this have anything to do with Teenage Mutant Ninja Turtles…so what is the point?)*

**Chris' Outrageous Cheesecake** *(Who the F\*\*\* is Chris and how did they get their own cheesecake?)*

**Dulce de Leche Cheesecake** *(What did the people in Latin America do to piss you off?)*

**Oreo Dream Extreme Cheesecake** *(Oreo's don't need any help. Sheesh).*

**Cherry Cheesecake** *(It's just cheesecake with some cherries thrown on. Shouldn't be offensive, but I'm keeping my eye on you).*

**Godiva Chocolate Cheesecake** *(Name dropping won't help here, buddy).*

**Hershey's Chocolate Bar Cheesecake** *(Even Coke and Pepsi can't be in the same restaurant).*

**Celebration Cheesecake** *(If your cat threw up a birthday cake…well, you get the idea).*

**Key Lime Cheesecake** *(Because Key Lime pie wasn't awesome enough?)*

**Tiramisu Cheesecake** *(Oh, let's piss off the Italians now).*

**Chocolate Mousse Cheesecake** *(Spoiler Alert: Does not contain real moose).*

**30th Anniversary Cheesecake** *(Wait, this crap has been going on for over 30 years?)*

**Craig's Crazy Carrot Cake Cheesecake** *(Who's Craig? Does he know Chris? Can he not commit between two different desserts? And why does he hate food so much?)*

As tragic as I think the actual cheesecake offerings are, I think my anxiety is largely tied to the menu.

The menu is a whopping 21 pages!

*Who has time for that?*

I watch people in line at McDonald's, staring at the board, unable to make a damn decision.

There's something like a total of eight items on a McDonald's menu. If you don't have that menu memorized from when you were five years old, there's no hope for you.

When you walk into a McDonald's, you know two things…

    1.  What you want to order *and*

2. You've pretty much given up on being healthy and said, 'screw the last five years of my life.'

That's it.

Clean.

Along comes Cheesecake Factory with its **250 menu offerings** assaulting your senses.

You CANNOT be good at everything. Seriously.

It's my responsibility, as a patron, to size up the restaurant menu and decide...

a) which foods you're going to suck at cooking in this wide range of multi-cultural frenzy or

b) if you don't move enough food and stick me with stuff that's just about to spoil.

At the end of the day, even with your 250+ culinary treasure trove, I order a cheeseburger and a Diet Coke.

# Motivational Posters

*"Hang in there, Kitty."*

*"Be Stronger Than Your Excuses."*

*"Some People Dream of Success, Others Stay Awake and Achieve It."*

I've had the privilege of consulting with some pretty heavy hitters in the world. Companies and individuals that are success personified.

They work hard. Play hard. They stay focused on their vision, despite the naysayers, haters, and detractors.

Oddly enough, I cannot recall one motivational poster in their offices.

**No** icebergs were talking about digging deep for strength.

**No** eagles flying over a shoreline, compelling me to stay above the haters.

**No** group of skydivers in a circle, touting the benefits of teamwork.

Nope.

They just seemed to have standard artwork.

**So, who are all these motivational posters for?**

**Losers!**

*Ok, that was a bit harsh.*

I think those posters are pretty cool. I also regard my 1976 Farrah Fawcett poster as pretty motivational too...but for different reasons.

**What the world needs are *realistic*, or at the very least, helpful, motivational posters.**

**Step One: Come up with a quote.**

*"Don't worry, the drive-thru manager can't live forever."*

*"At your ten-year reunion, that bitchy cheerleader will be fat."*

*"At least you were never invited to be on Jerry Springer."*

*"Do it! Wal-Mart jeans now have extra room for ankle bracelets."*

**Step Two: Add background**

Take one of the above quotes (or create one of your own) and put it on top of a spectacular photo of...

*...a sunset*

*...a mountain range*

*...somebody leaping over a creek*

*...an ocean*

*...a campfire*

*…a field of flowers*

*…anybody doing yoga*

## Ta-Da! - You've just created a motivational poster!

You're well on your way to a life of luxury, success, fame, and guest appearances on Futurama.

# WHY I SUCK
# AT INSTAGRAM

Every social media platform has a different tribe. Step out of line, and you'll stand out as the guy that brought a carrot-raisin salad to a frat party.

*First, let's go over the universal agreed-upon rules.*

Let's say you're merely drinking a chocolate milkshake, and you want to tell people.

**Facebook**: I like chocolate milkshakes. Leave your favorite in the comments.

**Twitter**: I've drunk a #milkshake #chocolate #bestdayever

**Pinterest**: Here are pictures of all the chocolate milkshakes I've ever consumed. #chocoholic

**YouTube**: I know people want to watch me slurping a milkshake.

**LinkedIn**: I'm an expert at drinking milkshakes. We should connect.

**Instagram**: Here is a photo of me drinking a locally sourced organic chocolate milkshake. #VintageFilter #GymLife #Organic #Chocolate #FoodPorn #ShakeLife

So, most of those platforms and the tribes that go with them are pretty self-explanatory.

There isn't really any undue pressure in interacting or deciding what to post...

...*except Instagram.*

**Instagram is all about photos.**

I don't know how many people I see at restaurants, stepping on chairs, making their partners get out of the shot, moving every item on the table to line up the perfect shot.

I want to play, but I spend an excessive amount of time staring at my food debating on whether it's 'Instagramable*'' in the first place.

*I'm pretty sure that 'instagramable' isn't a real word, but we're just going to run with it.*

So, here are my rules on whether you can share your food on Instagram:

CREATE FLOW CHART

Is this post about food? YES – Continue

Did you already eat all the food? YES (Do Not Post)

Does the food contain bacon, steak, a sunset, or water? YES – Continue

Do you need to use a filter to make it look better? YES – Continue

Can you think of at least 23 #Hashtags to go with the post? YES – Continue

Did you take a photography class or own a smartphone?

**If not taking a picture of food, then there are bonus points for...**

Are you also in a Gym?

Is there a sunset?

Can you also take the picture in front of a bathroom mirror?

*Note: You can follow me on Instagram @Godfadr – but don't expect to see photos that'll make you cry or anything.*

# OCD AND PEELING EGGS

I haven't kept it a secret that I have Obsessive-Compulsive Disorder (OCD).

Follow me around for a day, and you'll immediately see me check locks multiple times, repeat checks to determine if my car is in Park, and various items lined up meticulously on my desk.

**Most of it I can hide pretty well.**

*Some things…not so much.*

There are certain things I just won't (or can't) do.

For starters, the act of peeling hard-boiled eggs.

This is a disturbing practice for me that typically ends in the egg thrown down the garbage disposal in a not-satisfying-enough thud.

Saran Wrap is on the list of 'no-go' things as well. It pretty much just sticks to itself…and nothing else!

Now, that may seem like a mild annoyance to you, but if you ask someone I dated in my past, as chicken flew across the kitchen from being unsuccessfully wrapped…well…she might have a different story.

Saran Wrap always ends up in a ball of uselessness…

…and the intended item that was to be wrapped gets thrown in the fridge…completely unprotected from the elements and other foods.

**Do you remember that show *Monk*?**

It ran about eight seasons.

EIGHT SEASONS!

At the time, it held the record for the most watched [scripted] drama in an episode on cable.

*Think about that.*

Millions of people tuned in to watch Adrian Monk, played brilliantly by Tony Shalhoub, go through absolute misery each and every week.

Monk had a variety of phobias, but OCD was the most noticeable in the show.

I had trouble watching that show. To me, it wasn't funny. That dude was suffering…and I understood what he was enduring.

Thankfully I never saw Monk have to peel an egg or deal with Saran Wrap.

I wouldn't say that I'm a 'neat freak,' but everything is usually in its place. I'm not one who'll lose items very often.

Sunglasses are stored in a specific location, as are keys, Chapstick, my iPhone, and water bottles.

Tracy asked me one time if I could be more 'obsessive' about cleaning the garage.

That is the funny part about OCD…you don't get to choose what you're obsessive about…it chooses you!

Tracy is a champ for dealing with me over all these years. Among a very long list of too many things to mention, if it wasn't for her, I'd never get another hard-boiled egg.

# "Turkey Bacon"

If there is any single request I was asked when writing this book, it was to discuss turkey bacon.

Before we get into the history or how this demon "bacon" came about, we need to start with a primer.

I snagged this from Merriam-Webster's dictionary online…

**Bacon - noun**

ba·con | \ ˈbā-kən, *sometimes* -kᵊŋ \

**a:**    a side of a pig cured and smoked

*also*: the thin strips cut from bacon

*That makes a lot of sense. I like Merriam-Webster.*

### *Or so I thought until I got to 'b'…*

**b:**    thin strips of meat other than pork that is cured and smoked (see turkey bacon)

Webster is a jerk! Or maybe Merriam is the problem?*

*\*Actually, I don't even really know if these are people or just one person with a potentially snooty name. But I digress.*

I did find out that Merriam-Webster started in 1828. That leads me to believe two things…

1.    They'd have their shit together by now *and*

2. There's no F\*\*in way that there was 'turkey bacon' in 1828!

So, since you seemingly CANNOT trust an online dictionary, let's review a few rules of bacon club.

**Rule 1** – Tell everyone about Bacon Club!

**Rule 2** – Bacon should only be called 'bacon' if it's pork. Hogs should be celebrated for their sacrifices, and literature should be in line with that fact.

*Sidebar: I'm not saying Charlotte's Web isn't a great book. I'm merely asking if we can pause and think about the farmer's family for a second? #BreakfastMeatsCancelled*

**Rule 3** – Turkey needs to get some therapy and just be comfortable with being turkey.

## Open letter to Turkey...

*Dear Turkey:*

*Don't listen to the haters.*

*Technically speaking, you're probably the single biggest food with a holiday practically dedicated in your name.*

*Ask anyone what they're having for Christmas dinner and you'll get a multitude of answers including Ham, Prime Rib, Roast, Duck, etc.*

*Ask anyone what they are eating for Thanksgiving and they will all reply, "Turkey." \**

*\*Except for that really weird dude who lived next door to me in the '80s. Spam roll-ups still don't sound right.*

*So, there's no reason for you to be insecure and need to improve your social status by muscling in on other foods.*

*Remember what happened to tofu? Yep, almost never recovered from trying to be everything to everyone; tofu burgers, tofu fries, tofu bacon, tofu ice cream... Get the F\*\*\* out of here...JUST BE TOFU!*

*I would hate to see that happen to you, Turkey.*

*You're fantastic in your own right. You OWN Thanksgiving and the next several days of sandwiches and football games.*

*Sincerely,*

*Every other food (but notably, bacon).*

## So...what have we learned in this chapter?

There's no such thing as 'Turkey Bacon.'

There could be turkey strips, turkey roll-ups, turkey sheets, turkey slabs, or mashed turkey. There's just no such thing as turkey bacon!

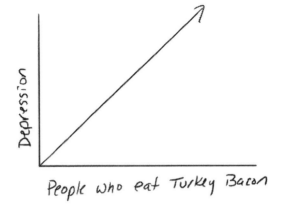

# SELF-CHECKOUT LINES

I love it when companies do something for themselves but try and spin it under the guise that it's a win for the customer.

Lowering the temperature of the coffee served didn't help me.

Oh sure, it sounded like a national safety move because some jittery 79-year-old dumps coffee on her crotch, but now I have to deal with cold coffee.

Purchase movie tickets online, and you get hit with a 'convenience fee.'

Yes, I printed my tickets online, but you, as an employer, didn't have to have some pimply-faced kid with buttery fingers and hygiene problems running the box office.

The worst one has to be self-checkout lines at grocery stores.

*This is for my benefit?*

*This is for my convenience?*

*I get to scan everything AND bag it up myself?*

*Oooh…how "convenient!"*

At the very least, I should get some employee discount for this service. You know…take 5% - 95% off my bill for the trouble.

The scanner never works for me. Plus, judging by the nasty looks I get from the 'self-service' checkout guard, I must also look like a high risk.

You know the person I'm talking about; he or she is typically in charge of a section of self-service kiosks because they failed 'door greeter' training.

They stand there replaying some questionable life choices in a daydream and, apparently, I'm going to take it out on them by stashing some beef jerky in my bag that I didn't scan.

Frankly, I'm not even sure how that security checkout scale works. HAL constantly tells me that I need to put something in or take something out of my bag.

God forbid I want to pay cash. That vending machine nightmare of not accepting any bill not minted in the last nine days is real.

Nope. Not one bit of this is convenient and these companies are just messing with us for their own entertainment.

I recently read an article where companies were testing the limits that someone is willing to be 'on hold.'

They call it the 'boiling point.'

Some sick bastard literally came up with a way to measure how much pain we'll suffer before we bolt and stop being a customer.

The answer, by the way, is 12 minutes in person and 13 minutes online.

I'm unsure where the extra minute of tolerance comes in…probably something to do with '80s hold music.

As opposed to just making sure we are happy – you know, dependable customer service – some companies are just trying to see how much pain we'll tolerate.

I highly suspect that the 'let's install shock mats in the self-checkout area' was vetoed at the very last second before these damn things started popping up in grocery and hardware stores.

I'd call and complain, but I really don't have 13 minutes!

# DOG PEOPLE VS. CAT PEOPLE

Not since pineapple on pizza and protecting Betty White from any natural disasters have people concentrated on such a vital topic…

**…dog people vs. cat people!**

*The critical thing to remember is that the dog vs. cat conversation comes with guidelines.*

Rule #1 – You're NOT allowed to like both. You must pick one or the other. Don't worry about which one you select. You'll have plenty of supporters and haters at your disposal.

Rule #2 – You don't need to own either to be involved in the argument. Gone are the days of needing "experience" or "insight" when getting into a heated discussion. Just jump in like God gave you the right to tell everyone the way it is!

Rule #3 – When making your case on why your animal is superior, working in a life-saving pet story will always be worth bonus points. You know, the dog woke you up when the house was on fire, the cat saved you from eating tainted tuna…whatever.

Rule #4 – If you don't have a life-saving story, saying your pet is a 'rescue' pet will get you bonus points as well. If you actually found your cat or dog in a dumpster…well…you pretty much just won.

Rule #5 – Proceed with caution if you're going to say your pet is an 'emotional support animal.' We're no longer judging your pet choice, we're judging you!

Rule #6 – If you dress your animal in clothes, and you're not living in a subzero environment, please let the adults run this conversation.

Rule #7 – Dog people must refer to their dog by namedropping the breed, such as "Labradoodlepug" or "Miniature-Chihuahua-Husky-Lab."

Rule #8 – Cat people must refer to their cat by color such as "white" or "orangish."

Rule #9 –Cat people need to be obvious when coming up with a pet name and stick to a corresponding color. (Snowball, Midnight, and Patches are popular choices).

Rule #10 – Dog names must align with a physical action (such as Rover) or an Action Hero (such as Hercules).

**So, with the rules in place, go forth and argue your hearts out.**

# Runners Are Crazy

We may not agree on the McRib, that the Green Bay Packers are really America's Team, or that Han shot first, but can we all concur that runners are crazy?

First off, the old joke is that they're always the ones that find the bodies.

You know, up early in the morning, running on some remote path that was visited by some serial killer only hours earlier.

**Runners' smug ambitiousness oozes out of them.**

Fancy shoes. Matching sweatshirts. Packets of gel goo in a fanny pack to keep them nutritiously fit for the challenge of running someplace that Uber has within its range.

Being smug is hard to pull off when you're not smiling...at all. I mean, have you ever seen a runner smile?

Oh sure, maybe they painfully grin ear to ear as they cross the finish line and throw two hands in the air (I think they just don't care). But the rest of the time, Ben Stein has more endearing facial expressions.

Of course, my big problem isn't that they wear colors that no man (or woman) should be caught in public with, ever. No, my problem is that they're burning precious calories.

I highly suspect there's a limited number of calories on this planet.

*I mean, it's just physics.*

**I've never seen a fat astronaut.**

So, it's safe to say that the world's calories don't float up to the international space station and fall to rest on the astronauts of the world…otherwise, they'd come back fat.

That means that calories do not exit the atmosphere.

So, when someone burns calories on Earth, he or she has to float around a bit…until one lands on someone else.

**Animals are certainly included in this.**

Yea, I'm looking at you, elephants, and rhinos* – you two clearly got the wrong end of this (fat) stick.

*Side Note: Rhinos are just chubby unicorns. #NoFatShaming*

Once we exhaust the animal world, which doesn't take very long, given how fast we are wiping them out, the calories fall back on humans.

I've had the privilege of traveling the world, so clearly trade winds have some impact. Those of us living in the U.S. are at a much higher risk of weight gain. Not because of what we eat or any personal responsibility – nope, just dumb luck of the wind.

Anyway, these burned calories float around until they find poor Skippy, minding his own business, watching Monday Night Football, or Karen, a model citizen, reading trashy novels on the back porch (that's soooo Karen).

Since they're stationary, they're easy targets.

The calories land on them and melt into the skin faster than The Thing absorbed Antarctic scientists.

**That's it!**

Don't take my word for it…it's just science.

If the masses ever figure this out, there will be a consorted effort to stop joggers and other sports enthusiasts from burning calories.

Maybe someone will invent some sort of 'calorie suit,' so they can wear the suit, keeping the calories from falling on them?

Or maybe a "Calorie Zapper" on the front porch?

I'd support that sort of thing. Maybe a Kickstarter project is in order…

…or maybe I should get off this couch and go for a walk?

Nah, let's go with Kick Starter!

# WHY IS "CHICKEN" IN QUOTES?

I don't know who took the following picture, but it haunts me.

### Why is the word "chicken" in quotes?

There's no good reason…and it scares me to think of the reason why it could be in quotes.

*Is it real chicken?*
*Is it a grammatical attempt at sarcasm?*
*And, why pick chicken and not steak for the quote gag?*

I attempted to find a good explanation and turned to the Internet.

Did you know that there are 543 quotes ABOUT chicken?

Well, I'm sure more people have talked about chicken, but at least 543 of them were famous enough for someone to immortalize their chicken musings online.

People like Paul Simon, Chuck Norris, Tom Watson, and even Ludacris.

Supposedly Ludacris said, "I find myself eating different kinds of chicken each and every day, even if it's by surprise."

Well, that didn't help much.

**Side Note:** I can't help but wonder what situation you'd have where it'd be a 'surprise' that you have chicken.

**"Hey Milton, what are the tasty chunky bits in this milkshake?"**

**"Silly Ludacris, those bits are chicken. Surprise!"**

*Yep…I think that would do it.*

**My online search for answers continued...**

**Chicken of the Sea** doesn't have the word "chicken" in quotes...and that's tuna...not even close to chicken.

So, if they aren't putting a chicken in quotes, why is this coffee shop in the middle of Area 51 going through the effort of...

Oh...crap...Area 51.

Aliens.

They're serving aliens.

Sure, they could've put steak and aliens on the sign, but then everyone would assume they're serving steak and chicken.

Anyway, if you find yourself there, try the "Chicken" chili. It's awesome. So is the "Carrot" Cake...but I'll leave that for another day.

# JARTS*

### *Or, Not Sure How We Survived Our Childhood, Part I.

Frankly, I'm unsure how more of my friends were not killed at an early age.

Don't get me wrong. There were a lot of stupid or questionable things done in my childhood, such as jumping off houses with makeshift parachutes made out of sheets, building bike ramps with shoddy materials, games of 'dare you to eat that.'

**None of those things compared to the dangers involved in a game of Jarts.**

If you're unfamiliar with Jarts, they're oversized darts.

Like. Really. Oversized.

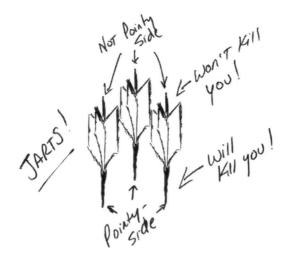

The object of the game is simple. You set two 'rings' on opposite sides of the lawn. The rings are small yellow hula-hoops made of plastic.

You're supposed to throw the Jarts in a "low arching trajectory" at the other rings.

Stick a Jart inside the ring, get a point. Whoever has the most points at the end of the game wins.

That's how the game is *supposed* to be.

Supply any child with a metal dart that's as large as the kid's head, and there are bound to be a few modifications to the rules.

**Height Bonus** – This was an added rule, by seeing who could throw the Jart highest. Getting closest to the ring was a bonus point. But, very quickly, the game evolved to where the rings no longer had any meaningful use.

**Close Part Two** – Closest to the ring was no longer relevant. How close you could get to your friend (without hitting them) was the most pertinent.

**Flinching** – How high can you throw the Jart, have it come back down at you at a rate of speed just above your level of coordination, and jump out of the way before it hit you?

**Vertical Sticks** – When you get to the point where the Jart landing on the ground gets boring, you move on to sides of trees, buildings, and metal sheds. Not real points involved, but ribbons were awarded for the sounds a Jart would make when connecting either successfully or unsuccessfully to an object.

**Flaming Jarts** — Since I'm not totally clear on the statute of limitations on childhood mishaps, I'm just going to leave this one to your imagination.

Like I mentioned from the onset, I still ponder how many more of my friends weren't struck down at an earlier age.

Thankfully, we didn't have any camera phones to record all of it.

So Long And Thanks For All The Bacon...

# I THINK I NEED
# AA MEETINGS

I'm pretty sure that my UPS delivery man is suspicious of my relationship with Amazon.

First off, in my defense, I'm unclear what constitutes a 'normal' amount of Amazon deliveries in a given week. Perhaps I need to start a poll...just to make myself feel better.

The speed at which Amazon delivers has put me on a path of becoming some sort of shopaholic and hermit hybrid.

When you can log on, order some obscure items and have them delivered the same day...well, that's just the age we live in currently.

There needs to be an Amazon Anonymous program for people like me.

*Me: "Hi, I'm Fred, and I've got a problem ordering too much stuff from Amazon."*

*Crowd: "Hi, Fred!"*

Amazon Anonymous probably needs a 12-step program as well – to measure our success rate.

**Step One:** Stop buying shit off Amazon.

**Step Two:** Here's your *"You stopped buying shit off Amazon chip."*

Ok, maybe we only need two steps...*but they probably get delivered to you via Amazon.*

When you lay it out in steps, it sounds so easy to quit, but delivery is soooo damn fast!

I mean, Amazon used to be 3-5 days. I thought that was fast.

**Then 2-day came along.**

Boom! I'll have that air fryer before Sunday's National Anthem gets botched by some pseudo-celebrity making a comeback on the fair circuit.

**Now the same day?**

"Hey honey, what do you want for dinner?" - Tacos...ok, let me 'same-day' some taco holders from Amazon just to dress up the dinner table.

I hear that Amazon is working on drone delivery.

I've started to take skeet shooting lessons. Attention! There will be prizes for anything you shoot out of the air.*

*I'm probably now on some watch list for that last comment.*

Chapter Update: Ok, I just jumped on Twitter and threw out a poll – just to see if I'm vindicated in my Amazon obsession. I asked how many deliveries people received per month. Here are the results...

**Fred Rewey**
@GodFadr

I might have a problem. How many deliveries from #Amazon do you get per month?

| | |
|---|---|
| 0-2 | **43%** |
| 3-5 | 14% |
| 6-10 | 24% |
| Don't ask | 19% |

*Suddenly I don't feel so bad. But to be safe, I won't bring eBay into the mix.*

# #TurnSignalChallenge

There are a lot of movements happening presently. Causes to fire us up and, presumably, better humankind.

Don't Eat Meat, Stop Vaccinating Your Children, Global Warming, Global Cooling, Getting Rid of Plastic Straws, Banning Civil War Statues, Stop Bullying, etc., etc.

Today, when you create a cause, you also need a #hashtag to help spread the word.

The most bizarre ones I've seen lately are…

#LobsterEmpathy
#PersonkindNOTMankind
#NotMyCheese
#StopRepresentingSnakesInANegativeWayInMovies

I'm sure some of these are significant causes…others…not so much.

I want to create a couple of causes we can all get behind. Sure, they may not fix things on a global scale like corrupt politicians or the burning of the rainforest, but I believe they can make our lives a little easier on an individual basis.

Now, if the past is an indication of future success, if you can wrap up these causes in a 'challenge' all the better.

Here's what I'd like to start…

**#TurnSignalChallenge** – A cause to encourage people to use turn signals when changing lanes or making a turn. Kind of like the #IceBucketChallenge, but this cause doesn't benefit anyone medically. Ok, maybe mentally?

**#DoNotTakeTheLastPieceOfPizzaChallenge** – I think this one is pretty clear and frankly, it's only directed to people in my house.

**#BaconRules** – I really don't know if there is anyone who can't get behind this challenge. Sure, maybe the people at #PETA will have an issue but beyond that, I think the rest of us are all on the same page.

**#ChewWithYourMouthClosedChallenge** – I mean, does that need to be a thing? *Oh yes, Virginia, yes, it does.*

**#FamilyThreeDozenWideInMall** – You know who you are. The rest of us are trying to walk around you and you are six-people-wide and hogging up the aisle. Just move the F*** over!

**#ElonMuskNeedsToAddAPizzaRollWarmerToTheTesla** – I think we know where this is going.

**#CigarsAreNotTheSameAsCigarettes** – I feel this one is important for non-smokers. The effort to ban cigars while simultaneously being ok with pot is crazy talk. I smoke cigars…in a lounge…not on your kids' playground. You don't see me walking over and knocking that White Claw out of your hand, so I want the same level of respect.

**#SaveTheGlutens** – I don't know what glutens are, despite my local coffee barista lecturing me on how bad they can be. I feel they're getting a bad rap and should be saved…you know…like Twinkies.

**#BanPoliticalPostsFromFacebook** – Might as well shoot for the top. More kittens, fewer donkeys, and fewer elephants.

**#HanShotFirst** – I think it's time we put this one behind us.

**#GoBuySoLongAndThanksForAllTheBaconBook** – I mean, if we're going to start spreading hashtags, this would be a good one for you to start with.

*…I'll wait.*

*…. Did you post it yet?*

**Thanks…you're awesome.**

**Lastly…**

**#IfYouAreOverSevenStopUsingEmojis** – Don't smiley face me on this one. You know who you are. You're a grown-ass-adult, so stop using cartoon characters to express any emotion I've no interest in receiving!

# EMOTIONAL SUPPORT ANIMALS

Some time ago a woman brought an 'emotional support turkey' on a Delta flight.

For those of you who are new to the 'emotional support' designation, basically, this is a function reserved for people with emotional issues. Basically, a traveling animal, usually a cat or dog, is suppose keep the owner calm.

For others, they can claim the pet is required for 'medical purposes.'

**Any animal can qualify, and the process isn't that difficult.**

Basically, a licensed mental health professional must determine that your emotional or medical challenge is disabling (such as anxiety or depression).

As for the animal themselves, there are no requirements. They don't need any special skills, nor are they required to do any tricks.

Typically, they're cats or dogs, but that does not stop people from getting and ESA designation for their furry…or not furry friends.

*Brutus is an emotional support squirrel owned by a guy in Florida.*

*Daniel is an emotional support duck.*

*A woman in Wisconsin has an emotional support Kangaroo.*

Monkeys, pigs, miniature goats, turtles, snakes, and hedgehogs have all made a list and traveled in style.

### Back to the turkey...

In some cases, bringing one of these animals makes sense to me.

What if there's some emergency? What if you crash land on a desert island and there is no food?*

*\*I originally typed 'dessert island,' which would be fantastic.*

**Careful planning and bringing your own food source could make sense.**

This is a proven strategy that goes way back in history. Take Noah, for example.

No one told Noah how long it was going to rain. He was just told to build a boat and get a bunch of animals together.

As the story goes, it was 40 days and 40 nights.

I'm not sure who was with him on the boat. Maybe some family or friends, or perhaps he rented out a few rooms via ArkBnB?

Anyway...clearly, he needed to bring food for this journey of unknown time frame.

### Did you ever think he just brought the animals along as food?

If it had been 80 days and 80 nights, we might have had a few fewer animals when it was all over.

I highly suspect that unicorns were the first to get eaten.

Oh sure, Noah probably survived off salads and grains for a couple of days…maybe even a week?

But then, while hanging with his emotional support platypus, he looked across the room at two unicorns and then glanced at his Traeger Pellet Smoker.

### *That was it!*

Two days later, there were Unicorn steaks on the dinner table, and no one asked questions after that.

I want an emotional support animal, but I desire something that gets me extra seating space.

When you fly some airlines like Southwest, it's open seating.

You usually have to resort to some pretty fun tricks to have people keep walking and choose not to sit next to you.

- Don't make friendly eye contact
- Don't shower
- Yell at an 'invisible' friend in the empty chair next to you
- Pop an Alka-Seltzer in your mouth (the foaming tends to keep people walking)

Those tricks should keep most normal people walking on by…but it's not foolproof.

Now, if I had an emotional support Honey Badger, it just might do the trick.

Does anyone know where I can find a Honey Badger and someone willing to give me an ESA designation?

I suspect a Honey Badger will be far more effective than my current emotional support beef jerky.

# DINNER WITH WHO?!

Sit around a cigar bar, a regular bar, Starbucks, or Panera Bread long enough with a group of friends and at some point, someone is going to ask the popular question…

**"If you could go back in history and have dinner with anyone who would you choose?"**

This seemingly innocuous question can be followed by lots of judgment. Who you pick says a lot about you.

The first time I was faced with this, I wasn't given the rules or the potential repercussions of falling into the trap of "one-up(ness\*)."

*\*This isn't even remotely close to being a real word and for the life me, I can't come up with an alternative.*

**Anyway, when faced with this "game," I choose Mark Twain.**

He seems relatively intellectual, funny, has no affection for politicians, and he smokes cigars.

*That answer sounds reasonable, right?*

Wrong.

Unbeknownst to me, there are really only two answers to this question.

First, you can say, "My Dad."

Presumably, this is reserved for people whose fathers have passed away, so they want one more moment with them.

Great, I chose Mark Twain, and now I feel like an ass.

I just wanted to have a fun evening filled with laughter and "Skippy" just wants to tell his father how much he loved him and to thank him for raising him.

## *Whatever!*

The other answer is the ultimate trump card in specific audiences.

"Karen" wasn't afraid to pull out the big guns.

"Oh me? I would want to have dinner with Jesus, no question."

Well, F*** Karen, I didn't know you could go that far back *(or go into quasi-fictional characters)*.

Now I feel like I squandered my entire dinner choice.

By the way…the game ends with Jesus. You can say 'God,' but that doesn't have near the credibility for some reason.

**Other people you can mention for a respectable response…**

- Joan of Arc
- Abraham Lincoln
- Winston Churchill
- Anne Frank
- Walt Disney
- Nellie Bly

- and Albert Einstein

**People you don't want to mention unless you're trying not to get invited next time…**

- Joseph Stalin
- Vlad the Impaler
- Ivan the Terrible
- Edward Cullen
- Mrs. O'Leary's Cow
- and that person who invented Crocs.

Yep, this game doesn't ever end well, no matter how you play it. However, I'm still sticking with Mark Twain.

# IMPOSSIBLE WHOPPER

Maybe I feel that I haven't upset the Vegan community enough with topics in this book, so I feel the need to weigh in on the recent trend of plant-based hamburgers.

As I write this, major "hamburger" chains have made the addition to their menu.

*Burger King – Impossible™ Whopper*
*A&W – Beyond Meat™ Burger*
*McDonald's – P.L.T.*
*Johnny Rockets – Garden Burger*

Also joining in on the 'fake' burger options are Carl's Jr, Freddie Frozen Custard & Steakburgers, Red Robin, TGI Fridays, Twin Peaks, and…wait for it…White Castle.

**We're nowhere close to seeing the end of this madness.**

Kellogg has even gotten in on the action with the Incogmeato™ (probably the coolest name out there) and Nestlé is following suit.  I do hope that it's chocolate flavored.

The ironic thing about these "burgers" is that some nutritionists have begun speaking out that they're not healthier. In reality, many contain more salt, more fat, and more calories – before you add cheese. *Or do you add fake cheese?*

I know what you're thinking, "None of this is funny, Fred."

**I know, right?!**

I was hoping for someone to name one "I Can't Believe It's Not Meat" or "Where's the Beef?" ... but no luck.

**If this all sounds a bit familiar, well, it is because it is.**

In 1973 there was a movie called *Soylent Green*.

The movie took place far in the future...2022 with Charlton Heston (Detective Thorn) playing a hard-nose detective after the truth.

To make the movie even scarier, it takes place in New York.

Due to a population explosion, people were provided what they were told was 'plant-based protein.'

It turns out, SPOILER ALERT, it wasn't plant-based at all.

*"The Ocean's dying. Plankton's dying. It's people. Soylent Green is made out of people. They're making our food out of people. Next thing, they'll be breeding us like cattle for food. You've got to tell them. You've got to tell them!" – Detective Thorn*

Recently some friends and I had a debate on Facebook over just 'how close' to tasting like a real burger these plant-based imposters are.

I must confess, as of writing this, I haven't tried one.

Don't get me wrong, I've every intention of trying one...I just can't get Charlton Heston's voice out of my head when I walk up to the counter.

I was told point-blank that it was "amazing how much the plant-based burger at Burger King tastes like a real Whopper."

*My response was...*

The question you need to ask yourself isn't, "Why does this taste so much like a real Whopper, but why does a Whopper taste so much like a fake burger?"

Look, I'm not saying they're made from people. I'm just not saying they aren't either.

SO LONG AND THANKS FOR ALL THE BACON...

# MIRACLE WHIP VS. MAYONNAISE

Since 1933 this argument transpired at just about every 'day-after' Thanksgiving meal.

I want to put this debate to rest once and for all.

1.  Use real **Mayonnaise** for anything you are going to eat.

2.  Use **Miracle Whip** to remove a stuck ring on your finger, clean piano keys, and removing gum from your hair.

Any questions?

SO LONG AND THANKS FOR ALL THE BACON...

# FRED MARKED HIMSELF SAFE

Spend any time on Facebook and you'll find a situation where people need to mark themselves "safe."

Of course, these are supposed to be reserved for some national disaster where communication is limited. You know, hurricanes, floods, tornados, etc.

**It didn't take long for people to create knock offs – less important 'disasters' to fill the timelines. Stuff like...**

*Suzy has been marked safe from windmill cancer.*

*Tom has been marked safe from watching Bird Box.*

*Karan has been marked safe from gluten scare 2019.*

*Doug has been marked safe from the war on Christmas.*

*David has been marked safe from Hurricane Sharpie.*

*Ed has been marked safe from Black Friday Sales.*

**For me, I probably need just to be marked safe from specific meals I've eaten.**

*Fred has been marked safe from the Chili Omelet.*

*Fred had been marked safe from 64oz of Prime Rib.*

*Fred has been marked safe from buffet bacon.*

*Fred had been marked safe from breakfast milkshakes.*

*Fred has been marked safe from lettuce.*

**Don't get me wrong, it wasn't all food-related. Some normal life things would make the list…**

*Fred has been marked safe from watching Son of Mask.*

*Fred has been marked safe from a Microsoft Update.*

*Fred has been marked safe from dude sitting next to him on a plane cutting his toenails.*

**What are you going to be marked safe from…in the real world?**

# TOTS AND PEARS

I am trying very hard not to have a list of rants in this book.

Don't get me wrong, spend longer than 20 seconds on social media and you will hear your IQ go down.*

*That statement is physically incorrect for so many reasons.*

So, for the purpose of being concise, I'm only going to target two things.

<Rant>First off, **Quotes**.

To keep the educational portion of this book simple, just know this...

## HE OR SHE NEVER SAID THAT.

Quotes you see attributed to celebrities, politicians, and sports figures; they probably never said that.

Here are a couple of my favorites...

*"Don't believe everything you read on the Internet just because there's a picture with a quote next to it." – Abraham Lincoln*

*"I never said half the crap people said I did." – Albert Einstein*

*"What's up M8?" – Socrates*

*"F\*\*\* Off or I'll punch you in the throat." – Mahatma Gandhi*

Personally, I think that last one could have happened on a bad day, but we will never really know.

My point is unless you heard it IN PERSON, it probably didn't happen. Believe it, or not...people make stuff up all the time. This is true ON ALL sides of the political spectrum – so don't think your tribe is unique.

The only other topic I want to talk about is this whole 'Thoughts and Prayers" thing.

I get it. We feel bad and we don't know what to say. People throw out a "Thoughts and Prayers" comment and then go back to their normal lives.

I just really think, for most people, it would be good to send over a message that is a little more positive. Uplifting even. Something to look forward to.

I think everyone likes Tator Tots. At least everyone I have ever met, faced with the "would you like French fries or Tator Tots" question at a restaurant will always pick Tots!

And Pears...well...we need something on the list for carb conscious people.

**City hit by a hurricane?** – *Tots and Pears!*

**Wrecked the car?** - *Tots and Pears!*

**Lost dog?** - *Tots and Pears!*

**Kid flunked out of college?** - *Tots and Pears!*

**Someone ate the last of the bacon?** - *Well, Tots and Pears can't even help that one!*

**Dropped a McRib Sandwich?** - *Tots and Pears!*

I know most of the people mean well but either do something to help or keep your mouth shut. Donate time, money, sandwiches…something. </Rant>

# IT'S A JEEP THING

I recently purchased a Jeep Gladiator.

This addiction is nothing new for me, as it likely makes number seven in my Jeep purchase history.

Each time I purchase a Jeep, there's a certain amount of customization that occurs. Who just keeps a Jeep stock and not make some 'improvements?' - Psychopaths, that's who.

Now, this isn't a "Jeep thing." I think it is more of a guy thing. We just need to add on stupid stuff to make it more 'ours.'

To illustrate a case in point, my 1973 Nova had amazing chrome wheels.

I am relatively sure in retrospect that they may not have complimented my green and primer paint job. Whatever.

Anyway, deciding what to upgrade isn't a cut and dry decision. It can influence which car club you can join, should you so desire.

Sure, you can add anything you want to the interior - short of Hello Kitty seat covers – and no one will judge you. The outside of the Jeep is a different story.

Chrome is always acceptable if you're going down the "pavement princess" route but certainly won't pass the "do you take that thing off road" discussion.

No, the big topic at hand is the size of tires and how high to raise (lift) the car.

Tires are pretty easy. I typically look for something that will go down the road with ease, but if a truck full of Moon Pies overturns in front of me, I want to be able to climb that glorious mountain.

Lifting the Jeep is another story.

You want to make it high enough to look bold and ready for a zombie apocalypse but NOT so high that everyone questions your manhood.*

*Let's face it, the higher you jack up that Jeep, the more people know you're compensating for something.

I want something safely between low-rider and full-blown redneck. Is there a **How-To** book for that? Maybe a Masterclass or YouTube video?

Till I figure it out, the Gladiator is just going to have to stay the 'stock' height – meaning, the coolest club I can join is the middle-aged* guys who hang out in front of Costco for free hot dog day.

*I am well aware of the generosity that I am giving myself by saying, 'middle aged.'

# Social Media Quizzes

I was a day late in writing this chapter because I went down the rabbit hole of Facebook quizzes.

Before I go into the specific quizzes, let's revisit the warnings about why you shouldn't take these quizzes...

*...They're just building data on you.*

*...The government is keeping you occupied and distracted.*

*...Mark Zuckerberg is bored and making fun of you.*

*...Your insecurity is getting the better of you.*

*...They're building a clone of you to take your place in 2030.*

**I'm not sure who 'they' are, but they certainly have an aggressive agenda.**

Anyway, there are some stupid quizzes out there...

*Which celebrity is secretly in love with you?\**

*What superhero are you?*

*Which tattoo are you?*

*What city should you live in?*

*What's your dream job?*

*Which <u>Friends</u> character are you?*

*Which <u>Game of Thrones</u> character are you?*

*Why are you single?***

*Which Disney Princess are you?*

*What food matches your personality?*

*Which pizza topping are you?*

*Please be Jennifer Aniston, please be Jennifer Aniston!

**Taking Online Quizzes probably contributes.

**Here's a list of questions that I believe should be asked once in a lifetime…**

*How did I get here?*

*How do I work this?*

*Where's that large automobile?*

*What's that beautiful house?*

*Where does that highway go to?*

*My God, what have I done?*

The fact of the matter is that David Byrne was way ahead of his time.

# HORSES AND HARLEYS

If your kid asks you for a horse, say, "Hell NO!"

*Really!*

Run, don't walk, to the nearest ice cream store…and buy them the store or strip mall…*but don't buy a horse.*

When my daughter was young, she started riding horses. At the time, that seemed as good of a hobby as any.

It wouldn't lead to sitting in the rain for nine innings of softball. It wouldn't require me flying across the country to see her favorite team. It wouldn't warrant getting up at 3:30 am to sharpen skates.

Nope, a horse hobby seemed pretty solid.

**Until we purchased a horse.**

When we 'rented' a horse, it was so much easier. Basically, the horse came along, for free, with the paid lesson.

It wasn't long before some evil horse trainer came into our lives and convinced us that she needed her own horse.

Now, I'm not going to lie; purchasing a horse isn't cheap…but it isn't as bad as I thought it would be. I mean, we were not looking to 'invest' in a Triple Crown winner here…heck I was looking for something that could moonlight at a petting zoo.

Anyway, the purchase cost was just the beginning.

**Did you know that horses eat?**

*Seriously.*

**Like. A. Lot.**

Typically, there are various phrases and colloquialisms in our society that we're unable to determine the actual source without much debate.

Terms like...

*Spare the rod and spoil the child*
*Cooks with gas*
*Foam domes*
*Wisenheimer*
*Drugstore Cowboy*
*Dizzy with a Dame*

BUT...the saying 'Eats like a horse?'

That comes from actual F***ing horses!

A horse costs the same as roughly ½ of a new Harley-Davidson motorcycle per year. *Not that anyone has done that math...repeatedly.*

If the horse's eating doesn't present enough problems, then there's this business of shoes.

One day my daughter came home and told me that her horse needed new shoes.

Once I got past a very strange visual, I realized she was talking about horseshoes.

"How much?" I asked.

**$120.19**

I don't know if horses wear Air Jordan's, but I highly suspect her horse did.

*Of course, I just smiled and wrote the check.*

About 60 days later, my daughter said that the 'Farrier' needed to come out because the horse had lost a single shoe.

By the way, "Farrier" is a fancy name for the dude that I was buying a new boat for.

I told her to find it, and I'd nail it back on.

**If I have to admit it, it wasn't all a downside.**

Having a horse postponed boys, taught her responsibility, and got us all out of the house more often (mostly to look for shoes in a field).

# BODY BY BACON

I often get asked amid all my bacon posts, how do I maintain such a great looking body?*

*OK, nobody asks that, but I can retell this story however the hell I want. You don't like it; you go write a book.*

While I do enjoy bacon, and yes, I've been known to post '7 seconds of Zen' which is nothing more than bacon frying in a pan. I'm also cautious what I eat during 'Non-Bacon Meals.'

It also seems that publishing 'Eating Journals' is a big thing in the health community, so I think I need to cash in on that action.

**Fred's Body Transformation Plan**

Monday…CORE DAY
Tuesday…CORE DAY
Wednesday…FAST DAY
Thursday…ICE DAY
Friday… LIQUID DAY
Saturday…CHEAT DAY
Sunday…CHEAT DAY

So, first off, you'll notice that Saturday and Sunday are 'cheat days.'

I don't believe you need to deprive yourself 24/7 – so enjoy your weekends guilt-free.

The other days are very specific. Here are the menu items you get on those days.

**CORE DAYS** – These are your bread and butter days. These foods should be a staple to good health and happiness.

*Bread and Butter, Bacon, Eggs, Bacon Pizza Rolls, Steak, Hash Browns, Cheese, Wine, Pizza, Tacos, Cheeseburgers (without lettuce), Egg Rolls, and a McRib (when in season).*

**ICE DAYS** – Any item that is, will be, or has been frozen.

*Ice Cream, Pizza Rolls, Cheesecake, Mac and Cheese, Chicken Nuggets, Enchiladas, Ice Cream Cake, Waffles, Bacon Pops (some prep required), Lasagna, and any leftover that has been put in the freezer.*

**Liquid Only Days** – These are some of the toughest, so pre-planning can help.

*Milkshakes, Beer, Single Malt, Wine, Champagne (if you are feeling fancy), Kool-Aid (if you are not), Bacon Smoothies, Taco Shakes, and Organic Green Smoothie (just kidding).*

Obviously, the key to any body transformation is to make the plan as easy to follow as possible. So, feel free to interchange any day or food.

# SHIPPING KITTENS
# AND PETA

I'm uncertain how many times I've conveyed this story, tried to set the record straight, or been insulted by some well-meaning cat-loving champion.

The conversion starts with, *"Did you really ship a kitten in the mail?"*

Did I ship a kitten? *Well, the answer isn't that simple.*

In 2012, I started a cigar company called Nomad.

I'd been smoking cigars for many years and a good friend of mine named Avo Uvezian was at the top of the game.

We smoked together several times a week with him, always prodding me to start my own brand.

After several years of his suggestions, I finally made a trip to the Dominican Republic – primarily for some fact-finding on what it'd take to make a cigar.

Frankly, I felt like the kid in the Make-A-Wish foundation.

There I was, smoking a variety of tobaccos and blending a cigar.

Now, when I say 'blending,' it was mostly me just telling the real blender what flavors I liked, and he (Victor) turned it into a cigar. My ability to blend was far off in the distance at this point.

Anyway, at the end of the trip, we had a cigar ready to go.

It was a straightforward perfecto sized cigar that I named the Fugitive.

When I came back, I officially launched my company.

I didn't need the money. It was a hobby. If I could sell enough to pay for my habit, all the better. If not, the experience that was coming from it was a blast.

For the first three months, I sold cigars direct to consumers.

I leveraged social media, was the first to put my actual Twitter handle on the cigar band, and word about the cigar spread quickly. Fortunately for me, it was a good cigar.

**Here's where the kittens come in...**

When I would mail the cigars to someone, I always added something else to the box.

A cutter, hat, lighter, stickers...something.

I felt like it was Christmas...and what could be cooler than getting something you didn't expect?

Well, I started to run out of ordinary things and began throwing in odd items.

Corks, pens, an orange...whatever was sitting close to my desk at the time.

Not long after I had my first interview. It was a podcast that had a pretty solid following. The hosts had tried my cigars, thought they were cool, and probably had no one else to do the show that week.

At one point during the show, they asked me, *"What was the oddest thing I had mailed with a box of cigars?"*

Without hesitation, I said, *"Probably a kitten."*

They laughed. I laughed. We went on with the interview.

It was not long after the show aired that I was contacted by various people online about my mailing a kitten.

How cruel it was. How could I subject a kitten to that? Did I not like animals? Pretty sure if hashtags were big at the time, then I would have gotten #kittenkiller.

Anyway, I NEVER mailed a kitten. It was a joke. But once it was out there, it had a life of its own.

A couple of months later, I was on another interview, and they wanted to give me a chance to clarify my 'mailed a kitten' comment.

They asked me, *"Fred, did you actually mail someone a live kitten with some cigars?"*

I responded, *"A LIVE kitten? No."*

The hate mail resurfaced, and I learned that sarcasm doesn't work in today's society and that Schrödinger would be proud of me.

# SECRET TO A LONG LIFE

I found an article about the longest-living people in the world.

Specifically, it took several different cultures (presumably with a high number of older people) and put together a list of their common traits.

**In no particular order, the top five traits were...**

*...Move Naturally / Exercise*
*...Manage Stress*
*...Eat Only Until 80% Full*
*...Stick to (mostly) a Plant-Based Diet*
*...Moderate Alcohol Consumption*

**I'm pretty much lucky I've lived this long.**

Well, that's not entirely true.

I don't feel like I'm a very stressful person...so I've got that going for me.

I don't drink that much...so score two points for me.

*Here's where the trouble comes in.*

I don't eat a lot of 'plant-based' items.

And by plant-based, I pretty much mean anything that doesn't include meat.

I'm reasonably sure that Pizza Rolls and Oreos don't make the 'plant-based' list.

If Star Trek and the Kobayashi Maru taught me anything, other than I probably needed to watch less television as a child, it was that you could change no-win situations at will.

*So, let's make our list.*

**[Fred's] Secret To A Long Life**

**Eat Bacon** – I mean this HAD to be on the list.

**Be Nice To Other People** – And not just those that have the same opinions as you.

**Unfollow People That Are Jerks** – You know who they are. They troll you on social media and comment only to insert their social agenda. Dump them!

**Smoke Cigars** – I don't know any cigar smokers who are stressed. #fact

**Use Turn Signals** – Because you can.

**Drink Wine** – I mean, that's pretty much fruit…and it's on a lot of lists.

**Put Your Phone Down At Meals** – One, it's rude to be looking at your phone during a meal. Secondly, people steal your food when you aren't looking.

**Do Something That Scares You** – Except eating uncooked chicken.

**Travel** – Seriously, see the world as much as you can.

That should do it.

Maybe this is a boring list to some people, but it sure beats the heck out of that other list by 'so-called' experts.

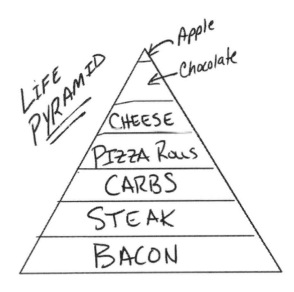

# TACO BELL AND THE ELECTORAL COLLEGE

Can we address Taco Bell at this point in the book?

What I mean is, we're far enough into the book that you either tapped out long ago and threw the book into the next garage sale bin, or you're still with me.

First off, I actually like Taco Bell.

## BUT...

And before you unfollow me on Twitter *(@Godfadr for a shameless plug),* let me at least explain myself.

I don't pretend that Taco Bell is in any shape or form *real* Mexican food.

Sure, they can dress it up in some commonly found Mexican ingredients such as tortillas or beans, but that's about where any real comparison stops.

### You want real Mexican food? Go to Mexico.

You don't even need to ask for Mexican food when you're there. There it's just called 'food.'

The next alternative to traveling across the border (the real one) is to stop ignoring that food truck you see in the auto parts parking lot at 1:30 am.

Chances are, those guys are pretty legit.

### *But with legit Mexican food comes a few caveats.*

As opposed to the English-speaking person helping you at Taco Bell, the food truck people may still be working on their English. Be patient, you're exploring another culture.

Next, at Taco Bell you'll find roughly two meats available on the menu: beef and chicken.

At the truck you'll encounter approximately three hundred and seventy-three. Ok…not really. But there are going to be 8-10 on the list.

This might not be the time for you to be all adventurous. This is probably the first time you're eating your meal ten feet from a guy rebuilding a transmission.

*Stick to the meats you recognize.*

### Now…back to Taco Bell.

As I said, I don't pretend Taco Bell is real Mexican food.

As Americans, we pride ourselves on taking any ethnic cuisine and f***ing it up beyond recognition.

I've been to Mexico numerous times. Not at any point did a waiter bring or suggest a "Beefy Fritos Burrito" or a "Jalapeno Popper Quesarito."

Those were real Taco Bell items by the way.
**Some other weird Taco Bell items include…**

**Double Decker Supreme Taco** – Basically, a taco supreme smothered in beans and wrapped with a flour tortilla.

**Cool Ranch Doritos Locos Taco** – Whoever came up with this one was either drunk or smoking something other than cigars.

**Double Chalupa Taco** – I mean if a single Chalupa taco is good (and I am not saying it is), then a double must be even better!

**Naked Chicken Chips** – With Nacho cheese sauce, of course. Sometimes Taco Bell doesn't know how to stay in their lane.

**Cheetos Burrito** – It seems that Taco Bell can't get enough of cross-promotion. So hey, let's throw some Cheetos into a burrito and call it good.

**Kit-Kat Quesadilla** – I have never seen this one, but there are some pretty valid sightings out there. Taco Bell's answer to selling more desserts. Melt some Kit-Kats into a flour tortilla.

Which brings me to the educational part of this chapter (and makes the chapter title all make sense) …

There's the ongoing debate on whether we should stick with the Electoral College when electing the President of the United States or if we should move to using the popular vote system.

There are some excellent arguments back and forth. That aside, *know this…*

**As of 2018, Taco Bell was voted 'America's Best Mexican Restaurant.'\***

*\*and THAT encompassed 3,000 possible choices.*

Maybe one day we should look at using the popular vote for Presidential elections…

…but at least as I write this, I'm not sure we're ready for that kind of responsibility.

# Grocery Shopping

I probably need to stop grocery shopping. The fact is, I'm not very good at it.

Don't get me wrong. I'd miss the Indy 500 experience I engage in when using a shopping cart. But the actual shopping…well…probably not the best use of my time.

Forgetting about the fact the companies like Shipt will deliver the groceries to our front door to more efficiently indulge our personal gluttony.

I over-analyze everything and confuse myself over which product to purchase.

**Something as simple as 'milk' goes down a rabbit hole of choices.**

Now, the easy part is ruling out milks that are indeed…well…not milk.

Almond, Soy, Asparagus.

Milk comes from a cow (or at a minimum a mammal).

I'm confident there are not people milking almonds in some foreign country. Or at least none that I've witnessed.*

*I could search the Internet for something like this, but I'm fairly sure that it won't be pretty at the end of the day…so let's go under the assumption that this isn't happening.*

Once you rule out fake milk, then you then have this whole percentage thing to address.

**Whole milk, half milk, low fat, nonfat, 2%, 1%, and skim.**

*WTF?*

I just want milk!

You know…for topping off a way-too-large-portion-for-an-adult of Captain Crunch (with Crunch Berries of course).

**So, whole milk must be ALL milk - kind of like 100% orange juice.**

Half-milk must be half milk and half…ummm…water?

Throw in low fat, nonfat, 1%, and 2%.

Those can't have much milk at all.

If I were a conspiracy theorist (the brochure looks fun), I'd think we secretly ran out of milk a long time ago.

Farmers are introducing these 'other milks' to keep us from finding out the truth.

They're just watering down milk in a back room somewhere next to a lab with the last remaining cow they're trying to clone.

Forget all those commercials showing happy dairy cows in a field at sunrise. Nope. We ran out of milk a long time ago.

**In the early '80s, people were starting to buy bottled water.**

I'm pretty sure this was an extra income stream for dairy farmers. You know, since they were already using water and all.

The water was supposed to be some magical spring water. You know, from a forest of fairies, or the middle of an ancient glacier.

I always thought some dude was in the back, making $2/hr. just filling the bottles from the tap.

**At the time, the number one bottled water was Evian.**

*Evian spelled backward is Naïve.*

Well, now they're just messing with us.

Nope. I probably need to stay on the sidelines when it comes to grocery shopping.

Those are just two products I struggle with, but the list goes on and on.

It starts with the milk that dairy farmers are watering down. If I wanted water, I'd be on the other aisle buying Naïve.

**Final Note: Can we at least agree that all those people drinking Butter Milk are weirdos?**

SO LONG AND THANKS FOR ALL THE BACON...

# T-SHIRTS AND VACATION MODE

Like a typical male, I have a closet full of t-shirts. To illustrate this point, I went ahead and counted them.

I own 136 t-shirts. 137 if you count the one that I'm wearing.

I wear five or six different shirts when I'm home.

**That's it!**

You'd think with the multitude of t-shirt costume changes available to me it would mean I'd go months before you see me repeat shirts.

I could lend them out to friends and create some bizarre version of *Fight Club* (but it would be T-Shirt Club because I don't want blood on the shirts I don't bother wearing).

Well, slow down d'Artagnan, that's not the way this plays out.

I wear the same five or six shirts over and over. The rest sit and gather dust.

No, really. When I counted them…they had dust.

The five or six I wear are comfortable, get thrown in the wash every couple of days, and are probably shirts that my wife would throw out if I left them unattended.

**First off, I can't blame her.**

Men don't have fashion sense. Like. At. All.

The comfortable shirt we like to wear every other day (and think looks awesome on us) is probably the same shirt a homeless dude uses to wash cars (or himself).

The only time more shirts come out to play is when we're traveling somewhere...like on a vacation.

At this point, I dust off the shirts and throw 14-57 t-shirts into the luggage.

### *Here is the stupid part.*

Even when I get to where I'm going, I'm STILL only going to wear the same five or six shirts that I wear at home.

Basically, a good portion of my t-shirts has traveled the world...and never been worn.

I need a better system, but when we travel, all bets are off.

### We become different people...or so we think.

Case in point, when I'm home my bath towel lasts 3-4 days. The washcloth by the sink? Same.

I'll use the SAME towel day in and day out for several days.

But...

.... when I go to a hotel, they need to make it rain towels, and I'll go through 3-4 a day.

### Why?

*I've no idea.*

It's not like I don't have more clean towels at home.

I'm not 23 with only one towel in my bathroom. I'm a grown-ass man with a closet full of towels…that match!

Nope. When we travel, we're different people. We demand decadence…even if we're not going to use it.

# HOLIDAYS

Today is **Columbus Day**.

Well, it's slowly being changed to **Indigenous People's Day** because...well...I guess some people are pissed off that Columbus got credit for discovering a country that already had people on it.

It's kind of like finding a $20 bill on the ground. I mean it wasn't your $20 since someone presumably lost it. So, it stands to reason that you both can neither celebrate 'discovering' it nor should you be able to spend it.

Don't get me wrong, American Indians got a lousy deal not long after that and 60 cities (so far) have stopped with any 'Columbus Day' honoring.

Without delving into politics too deep, people love to shoot (no pun intended) at "foreigners coming to this country" despite, at one time, their ancestors being a "foreigner" themselves.

**Now, there are also a ton of holidays that make sense that I think everyone can agree on.**

- National Bloody Mary Day
- National Buffet Day
- National Whip Crème Day
- National Bubble Bath Day
- National Bittersweet Chocolate Day
- National Bacon Day (of course)

*[It's about here that Fred realizes that he probably didn't need to type 'National' in front of all these days. But my publisher will be happy with the increased word count.]*

- National Milk Day
- National Blonde Brownie Day
- National Tater Tot Day

**But, if you look at the list of national holidays, some of them are downright specific...**

- National Football Hangover Day
- National Stephen Foster Day
- National Bubble Wrap Day
- National Don't Cry Over Spilled Milk Day
- National Middle Child Day

**For some of them, I don't want to know the details...**

- National Seed Swap Day
- National Create a Vacuum Day
- National Ding-A-Ling Day
- National I Don't Have An STD Day
- National Respect For Chickens Day
- National Put Your Keys In A Punch Bowl Day

It seems there's no shortage of holidays you can celebrate – if you choose to. Most of them are for crying or eating anyway.

I suppose Columbus should've discovered America, but then also spilled some milk or invented the Leftover-Thanksgiving-Meal-Bowl. It just might've helped him stay on the holiday list.

# HOT TAKES

Everyone has an alcoholic beverage they will no longer drink because, one day, it almost killed them. For me, it was tequila!

I've never found the perfect jacket or bag. I have closets full of both. None of them match.

If it's too late to drink coffee, then it's not too early for a glass of wine.

I have a 50/50 chance of putting a USB drive in the computer correctly, yet I only get it right the third or fourth time I try.

There's something morally wrong with having Foghorn Leghorn on a Kentucky Fried Chicken commercial.

Autonomous cars will cut down on the road stoppage due to highway shootings. The cars will keep going, and then the police can figure it out at the destination.

Alexa and Siri weren't the threesome I imagined when I was younger.

Grammarly now has 'Tone Detection' software, so I'm screwed.

Dear Hollywood, you try and remake the movie *Shawshank Redemption,* and I'll burn that town down.

If you don't like single malt, cigars, and bacon…we can still be friends. I'll just be the cool one.

# The Meaning Of Life

This is the 42$^{nd}$ chapter in this book.

*I'm sure you can figure out the rest.*

SO LONG AND THANKS FOR ALL THE BACON...

# EPILOGUE

I have a really short attention span.

If I were to put my work resume in this book, it would look like…

a) I couldn't hold a job

b) That I was pretty successful in lots of different things

c) I was just clueless as to what I wanted to be when I grew up.

It was pretty much the latter.

That's why you ask little kids what they want to be when they grow up*…if you're like me, you're looking for ideas.

*Except when my daughter, who was very young at the time, said she wanted to grow up and make license plates because they looked pretty. Thankfully, she chose a different trade.

There was a point in my life where I was doing a lot of acting and stand-up comedy. In the late '80s, I was able to share the stage with some of the biggest names in comedy.

Well, many of them were not big names at the time, but they went on to become household names before the turn of the century.

For me, stand up was always a hobby: a place to vent about the weeks' trials in front of people who paid to hear me. Weird, right?

I was never a headliner; I was always the guy who 'opened' for the other guy (or gal) that was really funny. That was ok, the pressure on me to 'be funny' was far less than on the headliner they came to see.

It was therapy for me. For the other comedians, it was real work...and they paid their dues. Traveling the country, living out of cars, playing tiny clubs in the middle of nowhere.

I was too lazy to do that part.

So, I stuck mainly to the West Coast, getting great gigs here and there and perfecting the routines at "open mic nights."

I put open mic nights in quotes because, for the most part, they were really not "open" mics. You could not just walk up and put your name on a list. You had to make the cut first.

My first open mic was trying to get into a club called The Other Café in SF.

Like many of the clubs, the way to get on the list was simple. On Monday you called a number and left your name on an answering machine. On Wednesday you called the machine back and listened to the recording to see if your name was on the list.

That was it.

I called every week for six months straight.

Finally, I heard my name.

I probably called the recording back a dozen times to hear my name again...to be sure it was really me.

I made the list. I showed up early.

The MC for the night was a woman by the name of Sue Murphy.

She met me in the green room and asked me how to pronounce my name.

She reminded me I had 10 minutes and asked what kind of material I was going to do.

I told her I had some bits about religion and grocery shopping.

She looked at me and said, "Oh."

"What?" I said.

She proceeded to tell me that stuff doesn't usually go over well, but hey, "good luck" and walked up to the stage.

As luck would have it, the night went great. People laughed, for the right reasons, and Sue told me (with a pretty surprised look on her face) the set was great.

Don't get me wrong, there are plenty of embarrassing stories, name dropping, brushes with greatness, epic fails, and behind-the-scenes mayhem. I'm just going to save those for another day – or at least not put them in print where someone can prove I said it.

For the next of couple years, I was able to hit the clubs regularly. Pretty much any week I called and left my name on the machine I was in.

I started to work the other clubs like The Improv and the Punchline. The Holy City Zoo was one of my favorites.

It was not only where I first met Robin Williams, but it was also a tiny and challenging club for a comic.

I don't regret never pursuing that life more...but I do miss it from time to time.

I've written two other books in my life (so far) and neither of those is particularly funny. One is on finance (yawn but needed) and one is on social media marketing.

Frankly, I'm really not sure this one is funny either unless you share some odd-sense of looking at things as I do.

Thanks for reading, thanks for buying the book, and thanks for being you.

At the end of the day, we all have more in common than not. I wish we could focus on that more in today's world.

From everything I've read, we only get one shot in this world.

For me, I don't want to leave anything on the table. I want to be on my death bed with no regrets and say...

***...So long and thanks for all the bacon!***

Made in the USA
Middletown, DE
04 April 2023

28205196R00099